Ladybird I'm Ready...
for Phonics!

D0207610

CALGARY PUBLIC LIBRARY

JUL -- 2014

Note to parents, carers and teachers

Ladybird I'm Ready for Phonics is a series of phonic reading books that have been carefully written to give gradual, structured practice of the synthetic phonics programme your child is learning at school.

Each book focuses on a set of phonemes (sounds) together with their graphemes (letters). The books also provide practice of common tricky words, such as **the** and **said**, that cannot be sounded out.

The series closely follows the order that your child is taught phonics in school, from initial letter sounds to key phonemes and beyond. It helps to build reading confidence through practice of these phonics building blocks, and reinforces school learning in a fun way.

Ideas for use

- Children learn best when reading is a fun experience. Read the book together and give your child plenty of praise and encouragement.

- Help your child identify and sound out the phonemes (sounds) in any words he is having difficulty reading. Then, blend these sounds together to read the word.

- Talk about the story words and tricky words at the end of each story to reinforce learning.

For more information and advice on synthetic phonics and school book banding, visit **www.ladybird.com/phonics**

Book
Band
4

Level 12 builds on the phonics learning covered in levels 1 to 11 and focuses on different pronunciations of the graphemes learnt in previous levels.

Special features:

repetition of letters in words with different pronunciations

short sentences with simple language

"Oh, well," said Maisie. "I could make a cherry pie."

So, she made a very big cherry pie.

12

13

Story Words

Can you match these words to the pictures below?

judge

cherries

Maisie

ice cream

pie

slug

16

Tricky Words

These tricky words are in the story you have just read. They cannot be phonetically sounded out. Can you memorize them and read them super fast?

said

their

so

could

oh

17

summary page to reinforce learning

Written by Catherine Baker
Illustrated by Ian Cunliffe

Phonics and Book Banding Consultant: Kate Ruttle

A catalogue record for this book is available from the British Library

Published by Ladybird Books Ltd
80 Strand, London, WC2R 0RL
A Penguin Company

001

© LADYBIRD BOOKS LTD MMXIV

LADYBIRD and the device of a Ladybird are trademarks of Ladybird Books Ltd.
All rights reserved. No part of this publication may be reproduced,
stored in a retrieval system, or transmitted in any form or by any means,
electronic, mechanical, photocopying, recording or otherwise,
without the prior consent of the copyright owner.

ISBN: 978-0-72327-548-0
Printed in China

Ladybird I'm Ready... for Phonics!

Monster Chef Contest

"Hurry up, bus!" said Maisie.
"I don't want to be late for the
Monster Chef Contest!"

She was in such a rush that she took the wrong bag!

At the contest, Maisie had a shock.

"This is not my bag!" she said.

"I can not make my pie without slugs and slime!"

The rest of the monsters had
lots of yucky things in their pies.

Maisie had cherries, butter and ice cream.

"Oh, well," said Maisie. "I could make a cherry pie."

So, she made a very big cherry pie.

The judge, Mrs Moppy, took a
bite of Maisie's pie.

She began to chew.
Then, she began to smile!
"Who made this pie?" she said.

"Me," said Maisie.
"Chef Maisie," said Mrs Moppy,
"Your pie is fantastic! Cherries are
even nicer than slugs!"

Story Words

Can you match these words
to the pictures below?

judge

cherries

Maisie

ice cream

pie

slug

Tricky Words

These tricky words are in the story you have just read. They cannot be phonetically sounded out. Can you memorize them and read them super fast?

said

their

so

could

oh

Ladybird I'm Ready... for Phonics!

Monster Dance Show

Maisie and Clive were getting
ready for the Monster Dance Show.

Clive was a good dancer.
Maisie was not!

Maisie kept on trying,
but she was too clumsy.

She bumped into Clive,
knocking him here and there!

Could they be ready for the show?

On the day of the show,
Maisie and Clive were on last.

"Relax!" said Clive. "Just dance to the beat!"

But Maisie could not relax.
Bump! Knock! Clive went flying!

Clive went BANG into a big drum.
He flew off!

Maisie went flying, too!

They came down with a bow.
The crowd cheered and
called out, "Well done!".

"Wow!" said Mr Dappy, the head judge. "Your dance was fantastic! You are MONSTER stars!"

29

Story Words

Can you match these words
to the pictures below?

Maisie

Clive

dance

bump

judge

Tricky Words

These tricky words are in the story you have just read. They cannot be phonetically sounded out. Can you memorize them and read them super fast?

were

said

could

there

called

Mr

out

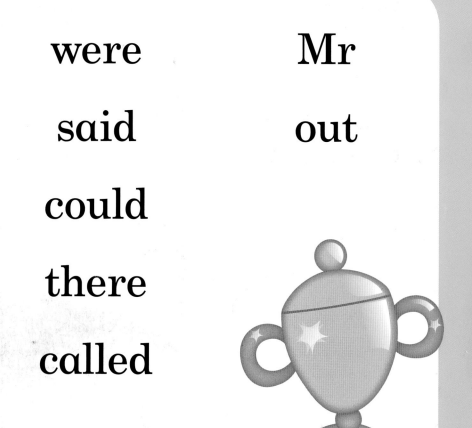

Collect all
Ladybird I'm Ready...
for Phonics!

Captain Comet's Space Party
9780723275374

Nat Naps!
9780723275381

Top Dog
9780723275398

Huff! Puff! Run!
9780723275404

Fix It Vets
9780723275411

Dash is Fab!
9780723275428

Big, Big Fish
9780723275435

Dig, Farmer, Dig!
9780723275442

Fun Fair Fun
9780723275466

Wow, Wowzer!
9780723275466

Wizard Woody
9780723275473

Monster St...

Say the Sounds
9780723271598

Flashcards
9780723272069

Ladybird I'm Ready for... apps are now available for iPad, iPhone and iPod touch.

Apps also available on Android devices